This edition published by Parragon Books Ltd in 2015

Parragon Books Ltd
Chartist House
15–17 Trim Street
Bath BA1 1HA, UK
www.parragon.com

ISBN 978-1-4748-0062-4

Printed in China

FROM THE MOVIE
Disney · PIXAR
INSIDE OUT

Book of Emotions

Bath · New York · Cologne · Melbourne · Delhi
Hong Kong · Shenzhen · Singapore · Amsterdam

THIS BOOK BELONGS TO

_____

_____

_____

When a little girl called Riley was born, her first Emotion, Joy, ran Headquarters from inside Riley's mind. As Joy watched what happened to Riley on a big screen, memories were created in the form of spheres.

Joy picked up the first memory – it showed Riley as a baby. It was gold because the sphere contained a happy memory. Joy placed the sphere on a shelf in Headquarters.

As Riley grew older, the shelves in Headquarters became full of memory spheres. Joy was also joined by four more Emotions – Sadness, Disgust, Anger and Fear.

Together, the Five Emotions helped Riley make important choices from the console inside her head. Joy was the leader and all she wanted was for the little girl to be happy. She was a big fan of laughter and chocolate cake.

Fear helped keep Riley safe. He once stopped her from tripping over a power cable when she was running through the house.

Disgust kept Riley away from things that looked, smelled or tasted gross. Like broccoli!

Anger cared very deeply about things being fair. All of Riley's tantrums happened when Anger was driving the console.

Finally, there was Sadness. Her role was not as obvious as Riley's other Emotions. In fact, Joy wasn't sure why Sadness was there at all.

When something really important happened to Riley, a core memory was created. Each core memory powered Riley's Islands of Personality.

There were five islands – Goofball, Friendship, Hockey, Honesty and Family.

When Riley was 11, her mum and dad announced that they were moving from their home town in Minnesota, to San Francisco!

The Emotions panicked! Riley had great friends and a great home in Minnesota. Things couldn't have been better.

After a long car journey, Riley and her parents arrived at their new house in San Francisco. Riley was miserable that she had to move, but Joy desperately tried to keep Riley happy by taking control of the console.

Before long, it was Riley's first day at her new school. Joy gave each Emotion an important job to do.

Joy was determined to keep Riley happy. She carefully drew a circle of chalk on the floor round Sadness.

"This is the Circle of Sadness. Your job today is to make sure that all of the sadness stays inside it," she told her.

At school Riley was asked to tell the class something about herself. Riley shared a happy memory of playing hockey back in Minnesota. But suddenly her smile faded and she became upset.

Joy saw that Sadness had touched the hockey memory sphere, turning it blue! As Riley cried in front of her class, her first blue core memory was created.

In an attempt to get rid of the new core memory, Joy turned on the memory vacuum. Sadness tried to take the memory from Joy but in the chaos Joy, Sadness and all six core memories were sucked up the memory vacuum tube.

They were sucked out of Headquarters
and dumped in Long Term Memory.
All the Islands of Personality had turned
dark, since the core memories weren't
in place to power them.

Joy knew they had to get the
memories back to Headquarters so the
Islands would work again.

But Headquarters was far away. Joy
collected up the yellow core memories
and both she and Sadness headed
across a bridge to Headquarters.

"But what if we fall into the Memory
Dump?" asked Sadness. "We'd be
forgotten about forever!"

"We won't fall," Joy answered. "Just
think positive."

Joy had just made it to Goofball Island when it began to crumble. It was collapsing because Riley had got angry with her parents and stopped goofing around with her dad.

Joy grabbed Sadness and they made it back to Long Term Memory just before the island disappeared into the dump. Sadness looked back at where the island had stood and realized that they could lose the other Islands of Personality, too.

Joy tried to stay positive – they would have to make their way to another island, through the winding shelves of Long Term Memory.

Sadness slumped to the floor in a puddle of despair as she thought about the islands collapsing. So Joy picked up one of her legs and dragged her along!

Back in Riley's bedroom, Riley was chatting to her old friend
Meg on her laptop. Meg told Riley about a new girl on the
hockey team. Riley missed playing hockey with her old friends
so the news made her angry.

At Headquarters, Anger took charge
of the console and flames roared
out of the top of his head.

Back in Long Term Memory,
Joy and Sadness heard a loud
groan as Friendship Island fell
into the dump.

Joy looked up at Hockey Island.
"We'll just have to go the long
way round," she said brightly.

As Joy and Sadness tried to find their way to Hockey Island they bumped into a funny-looking creature.

"You're Bing Bong!" Joy said excitedly. "You were Riley's imaginary friend!"

Riley and Bing Bong used to play together – they even had a rocket wagon that was powered by a song. But over the years, Riley had forgotten him.

Bing Bong told Joy that he was in Long Term Memory looking for a good memory so that Riley would remember him and he could be part of her life again.

"You know what? We're on our way to Headquarters. Come with us and we'll get Riley to remember you!" said Joy.

Bing Bong gave Joy his bag to carry the core memories
in and told them that it would be much quicker to catch the
Train of Thought to Headquarters.

"There's a station in Imagination Land," he said. "Come on,
this way!"

The three of them reached Imagination Land just as the
train pulled away, but Bing Bong knew how to get to another
station through Imagination Land.

Once inside, Joy and Sadness were amazed! There was
a French Fry Forest, Trophy Town and Cloud Town.

They soon reached a House of Cards, where Bing Bong
found his rocket wagon. They also found an Imaginary
Boyfriend Generator.

Meanwhile, Riley was at the try-outs for a new hockey team.

At Headquarters, Anger, Disgust and Fear tried to get Riley through them. But the Emotions couldn't replace the missing core memory, which meant Riley couldn't remember how to play. Riley missed the puck, fell over and then stormed off!

Inside Riley's mind Hockey Island fell to pieces and fell into the Memory Dump. Joy, Sadness and Bing Bong watched in horror from Imagination Land.

While they were inside Preschool World, some Mind Workers took Bing Bong's rocket wagon and threw it into the Memory Dump.

"No!" yelled Bing Bong. He sat on the ground and cried sweets. Joy tried to cheer him up, but nothing worked.

Then Sadness sat beside Bing Bong. "I'm sorry they took your rocket," she said.

After they talked about how he felt, he said, "I'm okay now."

Joy was surprised. Sadness hadn't made Bing Bong feel worse, she had made him feel better.

Joy, Sadness and Bing Bong finally made it to the train, but it soon stopped because Riley had gone to sleep.

To wake her up so that the train could start moving again, Joy and Sadness found a huge, scary clown called Jangles hidden with Riley's deepest, darkest fears. They led Jangles to Dream Productions, where Riley's dreams were made. When the clown crashed through Riley's dream she woke up suddenly!

The trio ran back to the train and jumped aboard just as it was about to leave.

Meanwhile, at Headquarters, Anger had plugged an idea bulb into the console. After everything that had happened, and without Joy around to help, Anger decided that the best thing for Riley was to run away – back to Minnesota.

After the bulb was plugged into the console, the idea popped into Riley's head just as she woke up from her scary dream.

Riley needed money to buy a bus ticket to Minnesota so she sneaked downstairs and took money from her mum's purse.

Back on the Train of Thought, Joy heard a loud noise and looked
out of the train carriage to see Honesty Island fall into the deep dump.
Suddenly the tracks underneath the train crumbled away and the
train crashed into the cliffside. Everyone on the train jumped off just
before it tipped over the cliff edge into the dump below.

"That was our way home!" Joy cried. "We lost another island....
What is happening?"

"Haven't you heard?" replied a worker from the train. "Riley is
running away."

After the train crash, Sadness had the idea to use a recall tube in Long Term Memory to get back to Headquarters. But as Joy got sucked up the tube, the cliff underneath them began to break apart.

The tube broke and Joy and Bing Bong fell deep into the Memory Dump! At that same moment, Riley was heading to the bus station, feeling nothing.

Down in the dump, Joy felt hopeless. She looked at a memory of a time when Riley had been sad but her friends had come to cheer her up. Suddenly Joy realized that Sadness was important – Riley's friends came to help *because* she was sad!

Then Joy and Bing Bong came up with an idea – they could use Bing Bong's rocket to fly out of the Memory Dump!

They sang loudly to power the rocket, but each time they flew up they couldn't quite reach the edge of the cliff.

They gave it one last try and, without Joy noticing, Bing Bong jumped out of the rocket so it could reach the cliff.

As Joy looked back she saw Bing Bong in the dump far below.

"Go save Riley!" he called. "Take her to the Moon for me, okay?"

Bing Bong then disappeared.

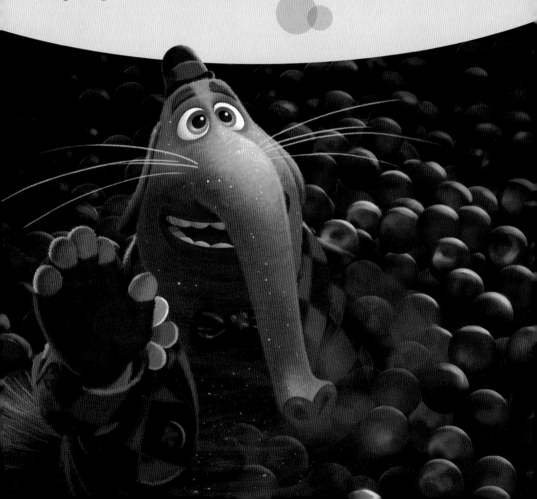

Joy had to get Sadness, who was floating on
a cloud, and get back to Headquarters.

As the Family Island crumbled away, Joy spotted
an Imaginary Boyfriend and had an idea!

Joy used the Boyfriend Generator
to make hundreds of boyfriends.
Using them as a huge tower, she swung
towards Sadness....

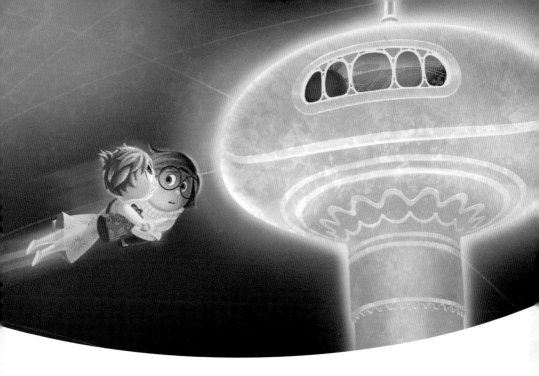

Joy grabbed hold of Sadness and the two of them flew
through the air towards Headquarters.

SPLAT! They hit the back window and started to slide down
the glass.

Anger, Fear and Disgust ran towards the window. How were
they going to get them inside?

Disgust had an idea! She got Anger really mad until flames
burst out of him and used the fire to cut a hole in the window.

Joy and Sadness climbed inside.

"Oh, thank goodness you're back!" cried Fear.

Joy looked up at the screen and saw that Riley was on the bus, ready to run away from home and back to Minnesota. She realized that she had to let Sadness drive and let her step up to the console.

Sadness took a deep breath and pulled out the idea bulb.
On the bus, Riley suddenly felt that she had to stay.
"Wait!" she called to the driver. "I want to get off!"
As the other Emotions looked on, Joy handed the core memories to Sadness and they all turned blue. Sadness placed them back in the recall unit.

Riley's parents were so happy to see her return to their new house – they had been worried sick.

"I miss home," Riley said as she remembered her life back in Minnesota.

Riley, Mum and Dad hugged each other and, at Headquarters, a brand-new core memory was created.

A few days later, the Islands of Personality had reappeared – with a few new ones, too!

Joy, Sadness, Anger, Fear and Disgust were excited about the future. After all, Riley was 12 now ... what could happen?

FROM THE MOVIE
𝒟𝒾𝓈𝓃𝑒𝓎 · PIXAR
INSIDE
OUT

Memory gallery

Riley's memories are stored in memory spheres. Add photos of your memorable moments to these pages. Use the coloured frames to link them to a specific Emotion.

Stick a photo of a
happy memory here!

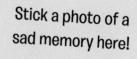

Stick a photo of a
sad memory here!

Stick a photo of an angry memory here!

Stick a photo of an embarrassing memory here!

Stick a photo of a scary memory here!

Family files

Riley's parents love and support her. Write about your parents and other family members here. Don't forget to add some photos!

Parents' names ....

....

Brothers' and sisters' names ....

....

Who makes you laugh the most? ....

Who is the best at helping you out? ....

Who makes the biggest mess? ....

Who gives the best hugs? ....

Stick a photo of
your family here!

Stick a photo of
your family here!

Stick a photo of
your family here!

How would your family
describe you?

. . . .

. . . .

Dream diary

When Fear is on dream duty, he watches Riley's dreams on the screen in Headquarters. What do you dream about? Do your dreams make you happy or scared? Fill in this dream diary.

Rate your dream

 for fun

 for scary

 for weird

Date _____

What my dream was about

_____

_____

_____

Date _____

What my dream was about

_____

_____

_____

Date _____

What my dream was about

_____
_____
_____

Date _____

What my dream was about

_____
_____
_____

Date _____

What my dream was about

_____
_____
_____

Magical memory

Joy takes pride in all of Riley's happy yellow memories.
What is your happiest memory? Write about
it on these pages.

When did it happen? ....

....

....

Where were you? ....

....

....

Who were you with? ....

....

....

What happened? . . . .

. . . .

. . . .

. . . .

. . . .

. . . .

. . . .

. . . .

. . . .

. . . .

. . . .

Friendship Island

Riley has to make new friends when she moves to San Francisco. Do you have friends you've known for years? Fill in everything you know about them here!

Name ....

What is their favourite film? ....

What makes them laugh? ....

What makes them cry? ....

What do they love to do? ....

Name ....

What is their favourite film? ....

What makes them laugh? ....

What makes them cry? ....

What do they love to do? ....

Name . . . .

What is their favourite film? . . . .

What makes them laugh? . . . .

What makes them cry? . . . .

What do they love to do? . . . .

Name . . . .

What is their favourite film? . . . .

What makes them laugh? . . . .

What makes them cry? . . . .

What do they love to do? . . . .

Name . . . .

What is their favourite film? . . . .

What makes them laugh? . . . .

What makes them cry? . . . .

What do they love to do? . . . .

Friendly faces

Use these pages to stick in photos of your perfect pals.

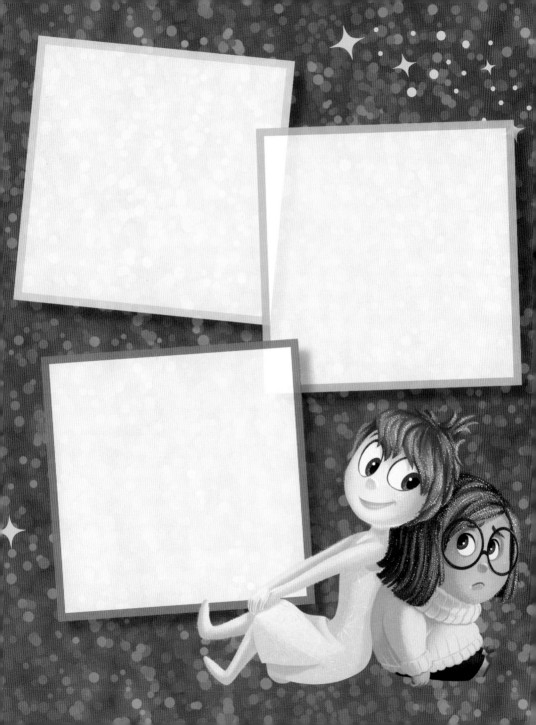

Memory dump

The Memory Dump is where Riley's old memories are sent when she no longer needs them. Use these pages to help you remember important things you need to do.

To do ....
....
....
Date ....

Done ☐

To do ....
....
....
Date ....

Done ☐

To do ....
....
....
Date ....

Done ☐

To do...
....
....
Date..

Done

To do...
....
....
Date..

Done

To do...
....
....
Date..

Done

Imagination fun!

Joy and Sadness meet Riley's old imaginary friend, Bing Bong. Did you have an imaginary friend when you were younger? If not, make one up!

Name of your imaginary friend ....

....

What does your imaginary friend look like? ....

....

....

....

....

....

What language does your imaginary friend speak?

....

What is the best thing about your imaginary friend? . . . .

. . . .

Who did you tell about your imaginary friend?

. . . .

Did you and your imaginary friend have a special song?
Write the words or make one up here!

. . . .

. . . .

. . . .

. . . .

. . . .

. . . .

. . . .

. . . .

. . . .

. . . .

Dream productions

In the Mind World, dreams are like movies. Are your dreams like movies? Write about the best dream you've ever had!

>>>>>>>>>>>>>>>>>>>>>>>>>

Where is the dream set?

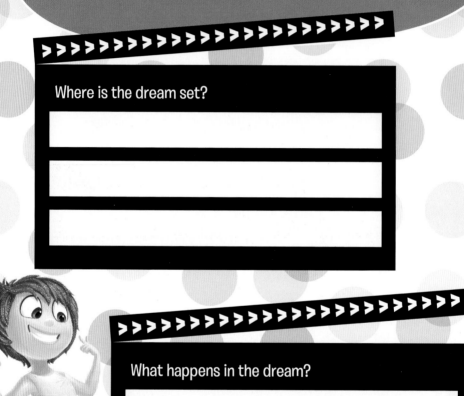

>>>>>>>>>>>>>>>>>>>>>>>>>

What happens in the dream?

Who stars in your dream?

When does the dream take place?

Idea station!

Have you ever had a lightbulb moment and come up with a great idea? Use these pages to jot down an idea when you think of it.

Road trip

When Riley's family moves from Minnesota to San Francisco, they go on a long road trip to get to their new home. Have you been on a trip recently? Write about it here and then stick in your favourite photos.

Where did you go? . . . .

. . . .

Place you liked the most . . . .

. . . .

Most exciting thing that you did . . . .

. . . .

. . . .

The strangest thing you saw . . . .

. . . .

Stick a
photo here!

Stick a
photo here!

Stick a
photo here!

Stick a
photo here!

Goofball Island

When Riley acts silly with her mum and dad, Goofball Island lights up. What kind of weird things do you like doing? Write about your goofy moments and stick in photos here!

Most embarrassing moment

....

....

Stick a photo here!

Silliest game you've played

....

....

Funny words you've made up

....

....

Funniest joke you've heard

....

....

Stick a
photo here!

Goofiest thing you've seen

....

....